The BIG BAD Mood

For my darling daughters Cherry and Zora, without
whom The Big Bad Mood would not exist – T.J.

Bloomsbury Publishing, London, Oxford, New York, New Delhi and Sydney

First published in Great Britain in 2017 by Bloomsbury Publishing Plc
50 Bedford Square, London WC1B 3DP

www.bloomsbury.com

BLOOMSBURY is a registered trademark of Bloomsbury Publishing Plc

Text copyright © Tom Jamieson 2017
Illustrations copyright © Olga Demidova 2017

The moral rights of the author and illustrator have been asserted

A CIP catalogue record of this book is available from the British Library

ISBN 978 1 4088 3919 5 (HB)
ISBN 978 1 4088 3920 1 (PB)
ISBN 978 1 4088 4804 3 (eBook)

All papers used by Bloomsbury Publishing are natural, recyclable products made
from wood grown in well managed forests. The manufacturing processes
conform to the environmental regulations of the country of origin

Printed in China by Leo Paper Products, Heshan, Guangdong

1 3 5 7 9 10 8 6 4 2

Tom Jamieson
and
Olga Demidova

The
BIG
BAD
Mood

BLOOMSBURY
LONDON OXFORD NEW YORK NEW DELHI SYDNEY

George was having one of THOSE days.

The sort of day when George shouts,

"I will **not** play nicely!"

When he stomps,

"I will **not** share my toys!"

And when he screams,

"I won't . . .

I can't . . .

I don't want to!

No!"

"There's a big bad mood
hanging around you today,"
sighed George's mum.

George glanced around.
There wasn't a big bad mood
anywhere near him.

Which meant it had to be somewhere else . . .

George looked under his bed . . .

At the back of the toy cupboard . . .

At the bottom of the garden . . .

But he couldn't find
the big bad mood and
that made George feel

rather big,

bad and

moody.

So he stomped

and stomped until

he couldn't stomp any more,

and then suddenly . . .

The **Big Bad Mood** was standing right in front of him.
He was a curious fellow, rough like sandpaper and
smelling of socks which REALLY needed changing.

"I'm the Big Bad Mood.

It's MY job to make
EVERYONE
big, bad and moody.
And YOU can help me."

So the Big Bad Mood grabbed George's hand
and off they went to create mischief.

First, the Big Bad Mood showed him how to make

The World Famous Big Bad Mood Sandwich.

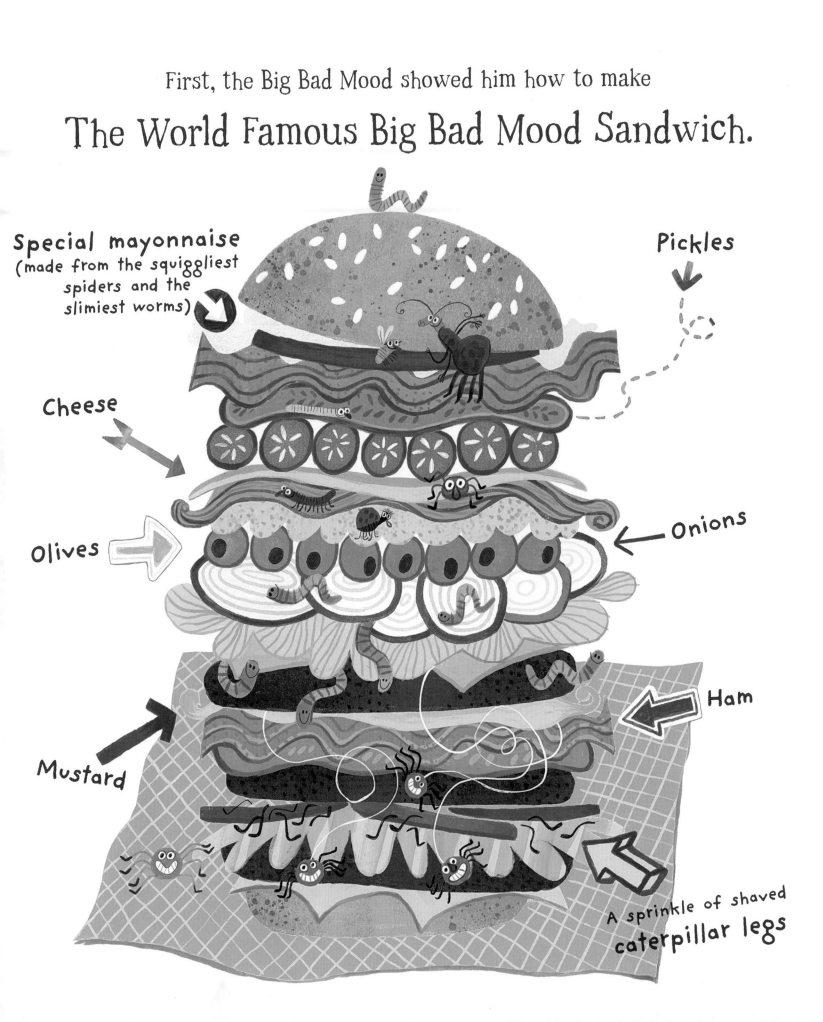

Special mayonnaise
(made from the squiggliest
spiders and the
slimiest worms)

Pickles

Cheese

Olives

Onions

Mustard

Ham

A sprinkle of shaved
caterpillar legs

Then they dressed up Mrs McTavish's seventeen slobbery dogs in her very best clothes and hats, which put Mrs McTavish in a big, bad mood.

And her dogs weren't happy either.

After that, George and the Big Bad Mood
swapped all the park benches
with trampolines.

(Which made the old ladies jump!)

They even filled the local swimming pool with
jelly and custard, which made everyone
not just big, bad and moody,

but a tiny bit delicious as well.

George and the
Big Bad Mood
stomped and
shouted

until they could
stomp and
shout
no more!

Well, maybe just a
teensy bit more . . .

"BRILLIANT!"

yelled the Big Bad Mood.

"We should do this forever and ever."

But George was starting to think that being big, bad and moody ALL the time wasn't fun.

It was silly

and noisy

and very tiring.

But, **worst** of all it was making his friends **unhappy.**

Did he want to do this **forever?**

"No thanks," squeaked George.

"NO THANKS? WHY NOT?"

"B-b-b-because no one will play with me," said George.

"Where I come from, no one bothers with friends."

"But having friends is brilliant!" said George.

"No it's not!"

And with that, the Big Bad Mood stomped off.

But George didn't follow him.

Instead he cleaned his room from top to bottom
(he even found his favourite rocket he thought he'd lost forever),

and he said . . .

And everyone played happily all afternoon.

Now George mostly has what his mum calls his "Not-too-bad-at-all days".

But every now and again, when a very special friend visits . . .

George enjoys a
BIG,
BAD,
magnificently
MOODY
night!